written and illustrated by
Mary Jane Begin

To my brother Kit,
who likes fishing more than Ferris wheels.





Hand lettering by Leah Palmer Preiss



Little, Brown and Company • Hachette Book Group USA • 237 Park Avenue, New York, NY 10017
Visit our Web site at www.lb-kids.com

First Edition: October 2008

Library of Congress Cataloging-in-Publication Data

Begin, Mary Jane.
When Toady met Ratty / written and illustrated by Mary Jane Begin.—1st ed.
p. cm.— (Willow buds)
Summary: Badger is very excited when his best friends finally get to meet, but neither one makes a good impression on the other as Toady fails at fishing and Ratty gets sick at a carnival.
ISBN 978-0-316-01353-6
[1. Best friends—Fiction. 2. Friendship—Fiction. 3. Toads—Fiction. 4. Rats—Fiction. 5. Badgers—Fiction.] I. Grahame, Kenneth, 1859-1932. Wind in the willows. II. Title.
PZ7.B388216Wh 2008
[E]—dc22 2007048372

10 9 8 7 6 5 4 3 2 1

Book design by Alison Impey

SC

Printed in China

The illustrations for this book were done in watercolor and pastel on Canson paper.
The text was set in Edwardian.

Dear Reader,

I found this really old suitcase in my grandma's attic that belonged to my great-great-uncle Ratty. Inside, I found a set of diaries and a little key. The diaries were filled with funny stories about Uncle Ratty when he was young and just getting to know his pals Badger, Mole, and Toad, whom you might know from *The Wind in the Willows* by Kenneth Grahame. The book describes their adventures as grown-ups, but nobody ever knew how they became friends. I asked my friend Mary Jane to retell the stories from Uncle Ratty's diaries. She even called them Willow Buds—in honor of my name! Here's the key to each of the books. . . . I hope you enjoy them!

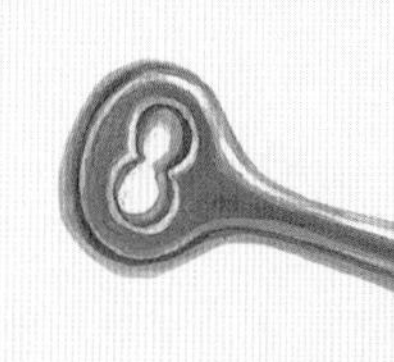

Your friend,
Rose Bud

LITTLE, BROWN AND COMPANY

New York ⤳ Boston

September 29, 1923

Dear Diary,

The smell of autumn is in the air, reminding me of the day I first met Toady. Badger and I had spent the whole summer fishing and all the while he kept telling me about his new friend. Badger finally introduced me to Toady and I felt sure we'd get along great. Was I wrong! Let me tell you the whole story.

Very truly yours,
Ratty

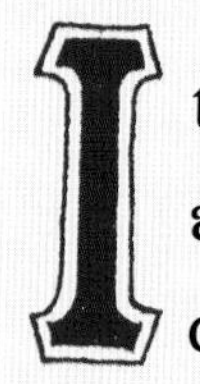t was the first time Ratty and Toady would meet, and Badger was very excited. Ratty had planned a day of fishing, and he and Badger could see Toady waiting at his dock as they rounded the river bend.

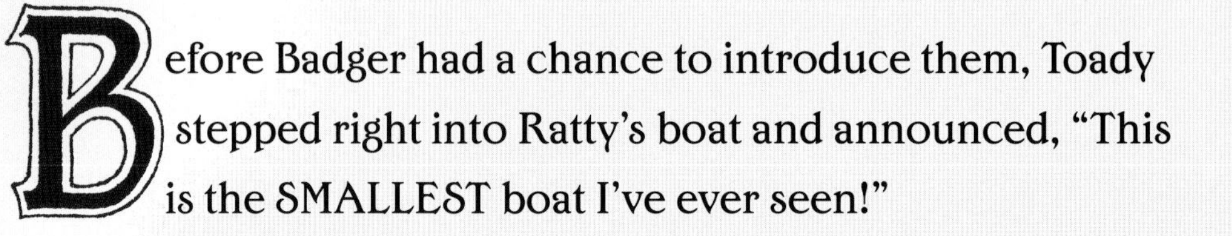

Before Badger had a chance to introduce them, Toady stepped right into Ratty's boat and announced, "This is the SMALLEST boat I've ever seen!"

Just then the dinghy began to sway, and Toady bobbed and tipped. Then, with a great SPLOOSH!, he fell into the river.

Ratty shook with laughter. "Toady, this is Ratty," said Badger as he helped a grumbling Toady from the water.

When they arrived at Ratty's house, they cast their lines into the water. After just a few minutes, Toady called, "Look! I've caught a big one!" reeling in his line as hard as he could. What he'd hooked turned out to be a muddy brown boot. Ratty tried not to snicker.

"That's okay," Badger said to Toady. "Maybe I'll catch the other one, and we'll have a fine *pair* of boots!"

When Mr. Ratty called the boys in for lunch, they stopped and counted their catch.

"I caught six fish!" declared Badger.

"I caught seventeen fish!" announced Ratty.

"I caught an old boot, a rusty can, half a yo-yo, and a rotten tree branch," said Toady miserably as he followed Badger and Ratty up the path.

s they munched their lunches, Toady had an idea. "Let's go to the carnival!" he suggested. "This is the last day before it leaves town!"

Badger enthusiastically agreed. As he and Toady began to plan the trip, Ratty grew very quiet. He was much happier in his comfortable little boat.

n the way to the carnival, Badger and Toady chattered excitedly.

"The cotton candy!"
"The Spooky House!"
"The Ferris wheel!"
"The roller coaster!"

Ratty felt his stomach flip over at the thought of those terrible heights and strange places. He wished he could turn the train around and go home.

Herald
5¢

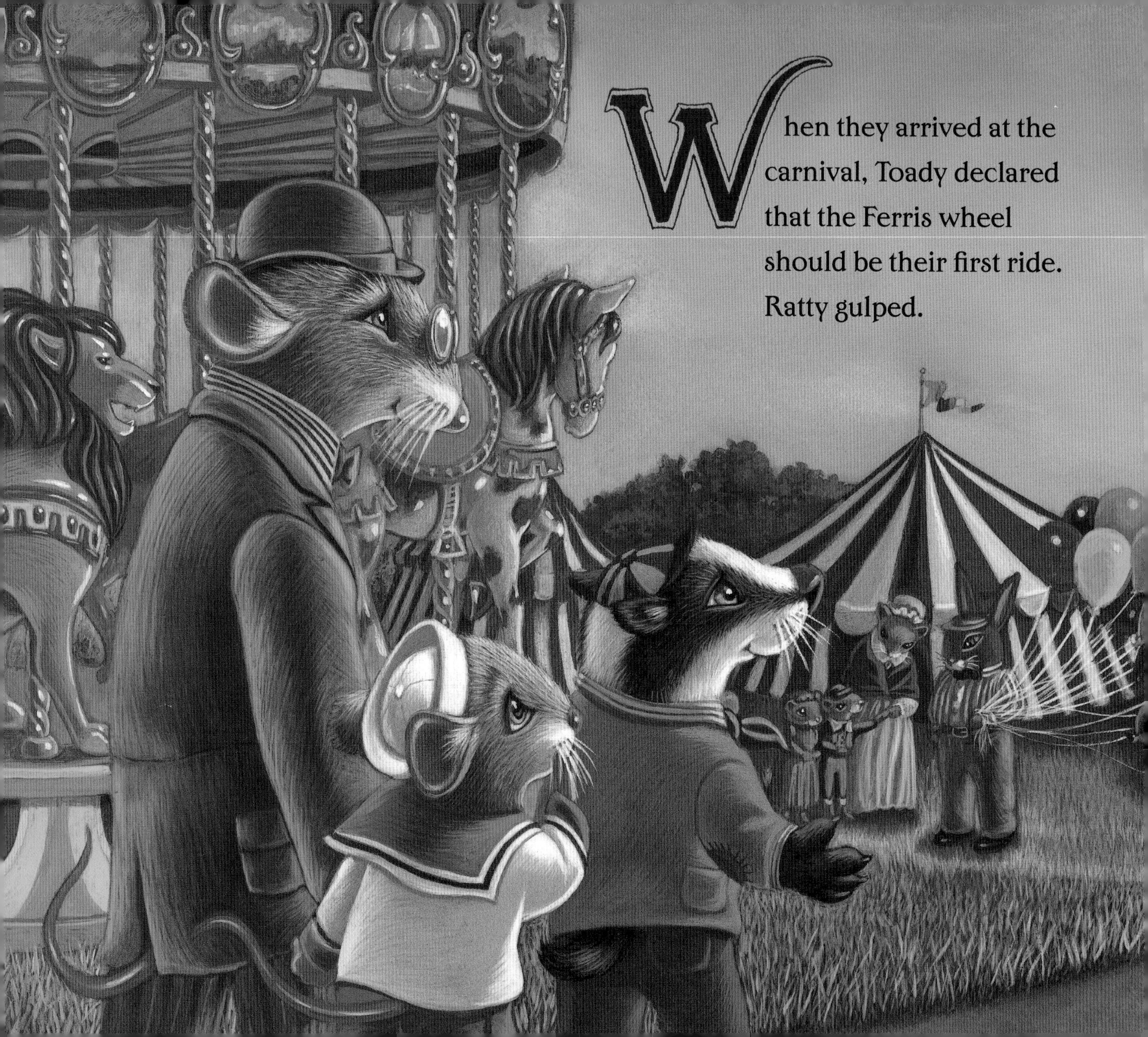

When they arrived at the carnival, Toady declared that the Ferris wheel should be their first ride. Ratty gulped.

efore long, he was slumping in his Ferris wheel seat, gripping the bar tightly as Badger and Toady rocked back and forth, hooting and shouting.

Badger finally asked Ratty, "Are you okay?"

"You're as green as I am!" Toady chuckled.

Ratty felt his insides roll sideways as he leaned his head over his seat. He knew what was coming.

fter the Ferris wheel, Ratty wasn't quite ready for the roller coaster.

"How about the Spooky House?" Toady offered.

"Sound good, Ratty?" Badger asked.

Ratty agreed reluctantly. Too embarrassed to admit he didn't like to be frightened, Ratty kept his eyes tightly closed during the ride—then his curiosity got to him.

He opened one eye.

Just at that moment, a monstrous mouth full of teeth lurched at him.

"AAAHHH!" screeched Ratty as he ran for the door.

"Hey Ratty," called Badger, "it was just a guy in a suit... see?" Toady followed in a fit of laughter. Ratty felt as tiny as a speck of dust. "I knew that!" he said as he turned away.

“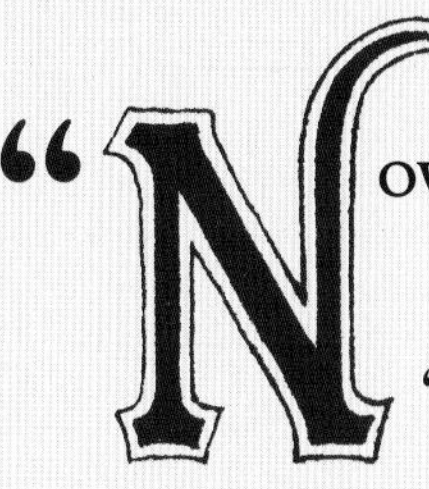ow, how about the carousel?” offered Toady.

“How about we go fishing back at the river like we planned?” replied Ratty.

“You’re no fun!” Toady shouted.

“YOU’RE no fun!” Ratty shouted back.

“You two are spoiling my day. I thought we could all have fun together.” Badger sighed. He turned from his two best buds and wandered into a nearby circus tent.

"It's your fault," said Ratty.

"He's *my* best friend!" shouted Toady.

"I met him first!" answered Ratty.

Just then, they heard Badger cry "CUT IT OUT!" from inside the tent.

Toady and Ratty peered in and saw a group of weasels circling their friend. "Hand over your tickets...or else!" one of the weasels threatened.

"We need to help him!" whispered Ratty.

"What should we do?" cried Toady.

Toady and Ratty spotted a horse tied to a pole.

"I'll ride the horse and you can follow," announced Toady.

"No, *I'll* ride the horse and *you* can follow!" declared Ratty.

"How about if I give you *both* a ride, and you can save your friend together?" offered the horse.

Ratty and Toady charged into the tent on the majestic mustang. Ratty held the reins while Toady shouted "YEEEHA!" and twirled a lasso as the weasels scattered in all directions. Badger joined them, leaping on a trapeze swing and whooping until the last weasel ran away.

"You guys saved me!" Badger cheered, jumping from the swing.

"Toady, you were amazing with the lasso!" said Ratty.

"I couldn't have done it without *you*!"
Toady beamed.

Badger climbed on top of the horse with his friends. As they rode out of the tent he said, "I'm so glad that I have two best buds like you."

"Me, too!" said Toady and Ratty at the same time.

"Make a wish!" Badger insisted. And so they did. Years later, they learned that they both had wished for the exact same thing. . . .

October 7, 1923

Dear Diary,

We each wished to have two best buds just like Badger had, and by the end of the day, our wish came true! Toady's a fine fisherman now, and I really don't mind being high in the air, ever since Toady took me up in his hot air balloon. I still don't like being frightened, but with two best buds to look out for me, I think I can handle just about anything!

Yours,
Ratty